THE PROPHETIC OIL

SAMUEL I. AKINDAHUNSI

ISBN: 978-1702658195

Email: samuelpublications@gmail.com

Phone numbers: +2348080659269, +2347010142868

TABLE OF CONTENT

INTRODUCTION

The Prophetic is the most abused and the most criticized of all ministry gifts as listed in Ephesians chapter 4. Everyone want to be a prophet or maybe I should say everyone want to prophesy. This is very good as the bible tell us it is good to prophesy, but because of error in the use of this gift, many don't want to even hear about it at all.

Also, many are called into the prophetic but they do not know how to go about it. There are lots of fake prophets out there, misleading people from the way of truth. Many people's lives have been destroyed because of false prophecies that were given to them.

There was a story of a man who suddenly packed out of the house, leaving his wife and children. He was told by a prophet that his wife was a witch and that the children have been initiated into witchcraft and that the wife wanted to kill him. This same man own houses, landed properties, fleet of cars and was doing fine. How his wife, with whom he suffered together to gather that wealth suddenly become a witch overnight is quite surprising. But he believed and acted on what he heard because it was coming from a respected prophet. It was later gathered that the prophet actually wanted to milk him dry and he had seen that the man's wife will not allow that to be possible for him, so he had to prophesy that the wife was a witch and wanted to kill him.

A lot of things are happening which is really placing a question mark on the prophetic ministry today. In those days, when a prophet speaks, people fear and tremble because they speak the mind of God and whatever they say come to pass, even kings and warriors fear them. But today, prophets have become people of ridicule in the face of the people.

This bad impression about the prophetic is what I intend to correct in this book. This book is also meant for prophets who have been called into the prophetic but are willing to learn the necessary information needed for them to do well as true prophets of the Most High.

This book will teach you how to flow in the prophetic, how to receive prophetic messages, how to deliver prophecies, how to hear and understand the voice of God the more and also, know the common mistakes of the prophetic ministry and how to avoid them.

I am fully persuaded that after reading this book, if you don't like the prophetic before, you will fall in love with the prophetic. Also, those who want to flow in the prophetic will also be activated to manifest this precious gift of Christ to His church.

After reading this book, you will prophesy.

Prophet Samuel Akindahunsi
Royal Message Ministries

1

A MOVE IN THE PROPHETIC DIRECTION

He that descended is the same also that ascended up far above all heavens, that he might fill all things.) And he gave some, apostles; and some, prophets; and some, evangelists; and some, pastors and teachers;

Ephesians 4:10 – 11

The prophetic ministry is one of the ministry gifts listed in the text above. It is a very powerful ministry with many things attached to it. The prophetic is also very delicate because it is very easy to cross into heresy if care is not taken; hence the prophet must be well versed in Scriptures and must have a correct understanding of the bible. It is a ministry of revelations, a ministry of power. Every true prophet operates in genuine power of the Most High. There have been several movements before the prophetic. The church of today cannot discard the prophetic. It is the prophetic that exposes things that is beyond the reach of natural knowledge.

There is a story of a man who went to the university and graduated with a very good grade. After so many years, he couldn't get a job and couldn't get through with his life. He was just moving from one problem to the other. Anytime he wanted to take a positive step, he would dream where an albino will be pursuing him. This continued to happen over and over again. After praying from one mountain to the other, one day he met a prophet. The prophet told him that his father (who was already dead), and his uncle did something in secret to help the man's education. This man was confused and he went to ask his uncle (who was still alive at that time) in the village about what the prophet told him. On getting home, the uncle told him that when the man got an admission into the university, there was no money to pay, so himself and the father went to meet a witch doctor for help, who told them to go get an albino that they can use for sacrifice so that the man's kolanut farm would yield in abundance. They did that and the man was given a knife and he was told to go mark all the kolanut tree with the knife. That year, the harvest was heavy on his farm. The kolanut yielded so greatly and he made more than enough money to send the young man to the university. So, it was the blood of the albino that was crying over the young man and that was why he kept seeing the albino in his dream from time to time.

You see, if not for the prophetic oil by which the source of the problem was exposed, that young man will continue to wallow in problem. Many people are praying without solution today, not because they don't have but because there are issues that needed to be specifically addressed before their testimonies can come in. The prophetic ministry is important in order to expose secrets behind sicknesses, sufferings and many unanswered prayers. We have moved into the movement of the sons of God where the prophetic should not be a scarce commodity in every local assembly.

The Ministry of a Prophet

The ministry of a prophet is more or less the most persecuted ministry of all, because the prophetic is the portal of the supernatural. The easiest way to enter into people's heart is the prophetic. Because many cannot hear God for themselves, the prophetic tears the heart of the people faster than any other ministry gift or spiritual gift. God uses the prophetic ministry to proclaim and to establish His counsel on earth. In the book of Amos 3:7, the bible says,

"Surely the Lord GOD will do nothing, but he revealeth his secret unto his servants the prophets."

So, the prophetic ministry reveals the mind of God to man. The prophetic ministry is like the intermediary between this world and the spirit world. It is the meeting point of humanity with divinity. Prophets are God's spokespersons; they are God's mouth piece. Therefore, the devil fights this wonderful ministry.

Prophets are called and ordained by God, but they must be activated by an already practicing prophet. This is the rule in the earth realm, except for some few when God step out of this rule maybe because there is no prophet around who can activate them and God is really in need of a prophet in that area. So in cases like this, God will use the available ministry gift to do the work of activation accordingly. For example, the prophet Samuel, he wasn't activated into the prophetic by a prophet because there was no prophet in Israel in those days and the word of God was very scarce. It was Eli the priest that helped him to recognize the voice of God when God first spoke to him. So, there must be a human agent who will help with this activation, which we generally refer to as impartation.

Also, note that anyone who desire to walk in the prophetic must be ready for criticism and likewise you must be ready to develop a thick skin against criticism because whether you like it or not, Satan will raise men to fight you strongly.

Now, you must know that this persecution is necessary and very important. Prayers cannot remove or stop it, because God will be using you to discover the source of people's problems and profound solution to long lasting problems and you shouldn't expect that the devil will be happy about that and fold his hands, while you tear down his kingdom. Therefore, he will come after you. But one thing is very certain: he will surely fall before you. Because before he comes towards you, the Holy Spirit will expose him and tell you what step to take.

Who is a Prophet?

A prophet is that man or woman who has close relationship with God and therefore has access to the direct information from heaven's library, either about people, nations or institutions. A prophet is one who has a special privilege to divine visions and revelations, among other things. The prophetic is God's spokesman. He is a man who reveals what God put in his mind. The bible refers to a prophet as the watchman over their territory. They have access to the council of Yahweh (I'll talk about this later in this book). The anointing of the prophet is the same Holy Spirit, but a different manifestation. The prophetic gift or the prophetic ministry is not gender biased, hence every born again child of God, whether male or female, have the full rights to operate in the gift.

Types of Prophets

There are two types of prophets: Nabi and Raah. Nabi are prophets who hear while the Raah are prophets who see – they are called seers. The Nabi hears by impression, God's thoughts, intuition, sensing and still small voice. The still small voice is not aggressive, but rather peaceful and calm. It doesn't push, it rather convicts. The Nabi operates through faith. They just take a step of faith and begin to operate. The Raah sees through pictures, open vision, closed vision, trance and flashes.

Virtues of a Prophet

The gifts of a man will make way for him to the top, but it is his character that will keep him there. More than the gift is the godly character that must follow so that the prophet will not misrepresent God. Gifts will attract people from different walks of life to you, but your character will determine whether they will stay or not. If you will continue walking in the prophetic and keep growing in it, certain things are expected of you.

1. A humble heart

Humility is very important to keep the prophetic flow. God despises the proud and nobody want to have anything to do with a proud man. Because of the abundance of revelation and knowledge, it is often very difficult for prophets to maintain a humble heart, but pride is very costly for a prophet. I have seen mighty prophets who are highly anointed, but they do not know how to talk. They address people anyhow. Sure, people will come to you because of the gift, but as soon as they have their miracles, they will leave you, because you don't know how to save yourself. A prophet must determine to discipline himself to walk in humility.

2. A quiet spirit

Psalm 46:10
10 ***Be still, and know that I am God….***

God speaks to us through our spirit, it is therefore important to maintain a quiet spirit. The Holy Spirit is a speaking Spirit who is always speaking to us, the problem is that we are not listening and that's why it seems as if He doesn't speak. If you want to hear God clearly always, lead a quiet life. To maintain a quiet spirit, you have to scrutinize what you hear and watch. Let the word of God be your daily meditation.

3. A consistent prayer life

The prayer life of a prophet is very important. If you see a prophet who prophesies deep secrets of men's heart and yet doesn't have a good prayer and study life, he's operating by a familiar spirit. If he's a true prophet, know that the gift have already been hijacked by the devil, because the prophetic cannot be operated without a good prayer or study life. Without a good prayer life, you cannot flow well in the prophetic because prayer will keep your spirit stirred and charged. The prophet must be an intercessor and must know that he's called to prayer for others as he is called to see beyond what others can see. So, he cannot joke with prayer.

4. Passion for souls

Passion for soul winning is another virtue of a prophet. The gift of the spirit is given to profit withal, that is, to win souls into the kingdom of Christ. So, the passion for souls must not be found wanting in the prophet's life. The more your passion to see people being made free, the more you will grow in the gift. God is looking for servants who will be more particular about what they will offer to the people His people, than what they will get from the people. These are the set of prophets who God is ready to open up to the realm of unstoppable growth in the prophetic. If you want more of God in your ministry, then let soul winning be the force that drives you when operating in the prophetic gift; Desire more to see people free.

5. An obedient heart

An obedient heart is also very important and even that a prophet should inculcate. Obedience is neither a gift of the Spirit nor a fruit of the Spirit; it is something that you must learn. The prophet must decide to be obedient to the voice of the Lord because a leap of faith will be required of him from time to time. He must get rid of critical mind because God will not always give him instructions that will be reasonable. A critical mind cannot walk with God successfully.

2

DIFFERENCES BETWEEN PROPHECY AND WORD OF KNOWLEDGE

For to one is given by the Spirit the word of wisdom; to another the word of knowledge by the same Spirit; To another faith by the same Spirit; to another the gifts of healing by the same Spirit; To another the working of miracles; to another prophecy; to another discerning of spirits; to another divers kinds of tongues; to another the interpretation of tongues:

1Corinthians 12:8 – 10

The gift of prophecy and the gift of word of knowledge are two different manifestations of the Spirit, which many believers mix together. It is important we know that, although these two gifts work hand in hand, yet they are quite different from each other. In this chapter, I will try to show us the difference between the two.

Now, it is important to know that there are certain things you cannot really teach except you are doing it. I am into the prophetic and I do what I am about to expose in this chapter. Some of it will challenge your usual beliefs or even question your religious mind. Only the truth challenges the status quo. I will therefore, speak to you by scriptures and by experience.

Many today who think they are seeking for prophecy are actually seeking for a word of knowledge. They want you tell them what they have not heard before about their lives or what only them knows about themselves. That is what they believe to be prophecy. Many today criticize the prophetic move saying, *"oh, is it biblical to call names, addresses, phone numbers etc?"* Some say, *"Giving details of people's life during prophetic ministrations is not scriptural."* Well, let me say that all these are scriptural and I will show you.

Jesus saith unto her, Go, call thy husband, and come hither. The woman answered and said, I have no husband. Jesus said unto her, Thou hast well said, I have no husband: For thou hast had five husbands; and he whom thou now hast is not thy husband: in that saidst thou truly. The woman saith unto him, Sir, I perceive that thou art a prophet.

John 4:16 – 19

Here Jesus described the marital status of this Samaritan woman. He told her she had had five husbands and the one with whom she was staying was not her husband (either he's her concubine or she wasn't legally married to him). That was an accurate word of knowledge, describing the marital status of the woman. It was prophetic and quite forensic because the next statement by the woman confirms it: *"Sir, I perceive that you are a prophet."* This shows that even the deepest secrets of the heart can be revealed through the prophetic.

Jesus saw Nathanael coming to him, and saith of him, Behold an Israelite indeed, in whom is no guile! Nathanael saith unto him, Whence knowest thou me? Jesus answered and said unto him, Before that Philip called thee, when thou wast under the fig tree, I saw thee.

John 1:47

Here, Jesus mentioned the state of Nathanael's heart. He was really a patriotic Israelite. It was an accurate word of knowledge.

And he sent Peter and John, saying, Go and prepare us the passover, that we may eat and they said unto him, Where wilt thou that we prepare? And he said unto them, Behold, when ye are entered into the city, there shall a man meet you, bearing a pitcher of water; follow him into the house where he entereth in and ye shall say unto the goodman

of the house, The Master saith unto thee, Where is the guestchamber, where I shall eat the passover with my disciples? And he shall shew you a large upper room furnished: there make ready and they went, and found as he had said unto them: and they made ready the passover.

Luke 22:8 – 13

Here, Jesus gave accurate direction; he told them where to go, who they would find and how to know he's the one and also, what to say and what the man would do. The bible says they found it exactly as he said it. That is the beauty of prophecy.

I can go on and on to show to you that the prophetic is real and that it is scriptural to talk about the details of people's life when delivering a prophetic word. In this chapter, I will show why knowing the difference between prophecy and word of knowledge helps you develop accuracy in the prophetic.

What is Word of Knowledge?

Word of knowledge is the presentation of facts about past and present events in the life of a person. It is the revelation of secrets through the Spirit. The word of knowledge is the gift of the spirit that helps the prophet to have supernatural access to truths that he did not naturally know or learn about a person, nation or institution. It always speaks of past and presents events only. A word of knowledge can come in the form of a vision, trance, dreams, impression, pictures or audible voices.

The word of knowledge is not the complete knowledge. It is a fragment of a body of knowledge. Only God has the complete knowledge. The word of knowledge is a fragment of a supernatural knowledge that you have no capability to retrieve or get on your own. It is through this gift that people call out names, addresses, locations and many other details as I have shown earlier.

What is Prophecy?

Prophecy is God talking to man. It is a revelation of the mind and intents of God to man. It is a supernatural communication of the mind of God to the people. It is a divinely inspired utterance or revelation from a yielded human vessel, aimed at communicating God's thoughts to His people. Prophecy comes through the mouth of a man, but flow into the man through the word of Christ. Every Spirit-filled believer should be able to prophesy, even though not everybody is a prophet. The Bible teaches in 1 Corinthians 14:31 that: *"For **ye may all prophesy** one by one, that all may learn, and all may be* *comforted"*. So every believer should be able to give prophetic declarations because every believer should hear God and once you hear God and you're speaking out what you're hearing from God, you're prophesying. Prophecy always speaks about the future. The simple gift of prophecy is speaking to men to edification, exhortation and comfort. We will still come to this later.

Knowing the Difference

Having said all that, it is now clear that the two manifestations of the Spirit are different, even though many mix it up. Prophecy is a speaking gift while word of knowledge is a revelatory gift; the two are very different. Sometimes, the two are mixed together and expressed interchangeably, yet they are extremely different. If you're waiting for a word of knowledge or detailed information, precision and accuracy before you prophesy, you will not do much in the prophetic; you will always miss God. So, the main counsel I will give is that you should learn to step out in faith. That is just the truth. The prophetic require you to step out and speak.

If you wait for accuracy before you start, you'll never get started and you'll never get it. Be bold enough to step out and speak even when you feel there is no word to speak. Names, addresses and phone numbers are all not prophecies, they are the word of knowledge. And for you to become more accurate in the prophetic, you must know the difference between these two and be willing to step out in it.

3

THE PROPHET AND THE COUNCIL OF HEAVEN

This is a very important aspect of the prophetic and I want you to follow it carefully. God does not want his children to be in darkness concerning any situation within or around them, but He want men and women who will be thirsty enough for the truth, to draw close to Him and hear His heart beat. God is willing to show you deep things about yourself, your world and things around you, but you must draw close to him. Secret things belongs to God, but will only be revealed to men and women who has a close personal relationship with God.

There is a place called the council of heaven or the council of Yahweh. It is the presence of God, where decisions are being taken over every individual, nations, kingdoms, territories, institution and the earth in general. Whatever is decided here is what will be done or carried out. This is where you will find the throne of God, the four living beings, the seraphim, the 24 elders and some angels.

For the purpose of clarification and conviction, I will show several passages of the bible, where this was plainly seen in place. You see, the bible never left us without witness to much truth, both the spiritual and the physical truth. Follow me into the bible to see this truth for yourself. After this chapter, you will glorify God for the gift of the bible.

John at the Isle of Patmos

The chapter number 4 of the book of Revelation described a sight that is very powerful.

1 After this I looked, and, behold, a door was opened in heaven: and the first voice which I heard was as it were of a trumpet talking with me; which said, Come up hither, and I will shew thee things which must be hereafter.
2 And immediately I was in the spirit: and, behold, a throne was set in heaven, and one sat on the throne.
3 And he that sat was to look upon like a jasper and a sardine stone: and there was a rainbow round about the throne, in sight like unto an emerald.

4 And round about the throne were four and twenty seats: and upon the seats I saw four and twenty elders sitting, clothed in white raiment; and they had on their heads crowns of gold.

5 And out of the throne proceeded lightnings and thunderings and voices: and there were seven lamps of fire burning before the throne, which are the seven Spirits of God.

6 And before the throne there was a sea of glass like unto crystal: and in the midst of the throne, and round about the throne, were four beasts full of eyes before and behind.

7 And the first beast was like a lion, and the second beast like a calf, and the third beast had a face as a man, and the fourth beast was like a flying eagle.

8 ¶ And the four beasts had each of them six wings about him; and they were full of eyes within: and they rest not day and night, saying, Holy, holy, holy, Lord God Almighty, which was, and is, and is to come.

9 And when those beasts give glory and honour and thanks to him that sat on the throne, who liveth forever and ever,

10 The four and twenty elders fall down before him that sat on the throne, and worship him that liveth forever and ever, and cast their crowns before the throne, saying,

11 Thou art worthy, O Lord, to receive glory and honour and power: for thou hast created all things, and for thy pleasure they are and were created.

John 4:1 - 11

The apostle John here described a great wonder. By this insightful account, we come to know that there is a gathering called the council of God. It is where matters are being discussed and appropriate decisions are being taken. The council of heaven is a place of several witnesses. The decision taken here influences the course of humanity and individuals.

We see here how God took John into the place of revelation where things that have been sealed for ages were revealed unto him. He saw into the future, even things that are hidden for ages. Mysteries were revealed to him because he was in the council of heaven where no secret remain a secret.

Prophet Micaiah before King Ahab

The king was to go to the battle. He called all his prophets and they all told him he could go. The prophet Micaiah was summoned and he was able to see, the meeting that was held in the council of heaven concerning the battle and also saw what would become of the king if he should go for that battle. Note that four hundred prophets had spoken before he was brought in and none of them were able to see what Micaiah saw, because they were not given the privilege of seeing into the council of heaven and hear the decision of the council over the situation.

We see this story in the book of 1Kings 22:19 – 22,

And he said, Hear thou therefore the word of the LORD: I saw the LORD sitting on his throne, and all the host of heaven standing by him on his right hand and on his left. And the LORD said, Who shall persuade Ahab, that he may go up and fall at Ramothgilead? And one said on this manner, and another said on that manner. And there came forth a spirit, and stood before the LORD, and said, I will persuade him. And the LORD said unto him, Wherewith? And he said, I will go forth, and I will be a lying spirit in the mouth of all his prophets. And he said, Thou shalt persuade him, and prevail also: go forth, and do so.

He saw exactly what happened and he proclaimed it and it was so. He was able to see into the unseen environment where the meeting was held and the decision was taken.

He was so sure of the prophecy that he then said,

"…If thou return at all in peace, the LORD hath not spoken by me. And he said, Hearken, O people, every one of you."

1Kings 22:28

This place where God and the host of heaven decide the fate of men, nations and institutions is what I call the council of heaven.

Angel Gabriel before Zechariah

When Gabriel came to tell Zechariah about heaven's decision to give him a baby boy, Zechariah doubted it and the angel said, ***"I am Gabriel that stand in the presence of God; and am sent to speak unto thee, and to shew thee these glad tidings."*** - Luke 1:19. What Gabriel was indirectly saying is that he was in the presence of God when that decision was taken and he was the one given the assignment to pass the message across to Zechariah.

A prophet can also function in this capacity, depending on their relationship with God. When you enter into this particular realm of the prophetic, you speak and nobody can change it. You don't have to pray to enforce such prophetic declarations, but rather, you speak the already concluded decisions about things. In as much as nobody can change God's plan, things revealed from the council of heaven cannot be altered by any man. The council of heaven should be one of the greatest desires of a prophet of God.

4

THE FOUR STREAMS OF PROPHECY

The prophetic ministry is beyond prophesying. We have the deep, deeper and deepest realms of the prophetic. The streams of the prophetic ministry can be divided into four: Spirit of Prophecy, Gift of Prophecy, Prophetic ministry and the Prophetic Office. All these four dimensions are powered by the self same Spirit of Christ.

Let me quickly say this, *"that someone is prophesying doesn't make him or her a prophet"*. As far as the prophetic realms are concerned, any believer can operate from there. But that doesn't make them a prophet; neither does it put them in the seat or the office of a prophet. We have to understand this basic truth. We will talk extensively about this in this very chapter.

Who Can Prophesy?

At this junction, I will like to emphasize this truth: ***"every believer can prophesy."*** As long as you are a child of God and you're filled with the Holy Ghost, you can prophesy. The prophetic is not restricted to some set of people as many suppose. When Christ died on the cross, the veil on the holiest of holies were torn, which is symbolic of the fact that any believer now have access to all spiritual blessings in the heavenlies.

Using the Corinthian church as case study, I can say that every believer can prophesy. The Corinthian church manifested the nine gifts of the Holy Ghost. The manifestations of the Spirit were not restricted to the pastors, elders or deacons in that assembly, all of them operated so well in the spiritual gifts. This is a pointer to the fact that the manifestations of the Spirit are not restricted to the people in ministry alone. Also, Philip's daughters in Acts of Apostles chapter 21 were not into ministry, but they prophesied.

8 And the next day we that were of Paul's company departed, and came unto Caesarea: and we entered into the house of Philip the evangelist, which was one of the seven; and abode with him.

9 And the same man had four daughters, virgins, which did prophesy.

Acts of Apostles 21:8 - 9

Again, Joel 2:28 – 29 says,

28 And it shall come to pass afterward, that I will pour out my spirit upon all flesh; and your sons and your daughters shall prophesy, your old men shall dream dreams, your young men shall see visions:
29 And also upon the servants and upon the handmaids in those days will I pour out my spirit.

Here, God said he would pour out His Spirit upon all flesh and sons and daughters shall prophesy. Note that He never said only prophets shall prophesy. Nevertheless, the office of a prophet is still more superior to any of the other manifestations of the prophetic.

The Spirit of Prophecy

This is the simplest level of the prophetic. This is the realm where the Spirit of God takes over an available human vessel to speak in the gathering of the brethren. It is never premeditated by the vessel. A man that is used by God in this direction is not a prophet. This is where many people miss it; they start calling themselves prophets simple because they prophesy through the Spirit of prophecy.

Because God cannot be hindered and cannot be stopped, if He wants to give a message to His people in a gathering and a prophet is not available, He rests on an available vessel and say whatever He want to say. However, we must understand that this singular act does not make the person a prophet. At that moment, the person used is only a prophetic servant and this person may never prophesy again in their lifetime. It is not a gift and therefore isn't resident in the vessel at all. The manifestation comes and goes. We must also know that the in the case of the Spirit of prophecy, the choice of who to be used solely depends on the Holy Spirit who chooses who He wills, so no man can chose to be used in this respect.

The Gift of Prophecy

This is the gift mentioned in 1Corinthians 12. It is the manifestation of the Holy Ghost through a vessel. It is a gift and therefore, it is resident in the person. The carrier can switch it on and off. The gift of prophecy is what God gives you and you are able to speak forth in word of prophecy. It is also the same manifestation of the Holy Spirit, yet the carrier is not therefore, a prophet. This is because he is not seated in that realm. The function of the Spirit and gift of prophecy is similar. According to 1Corinthians 14:3, ***"But he that prophesieth speaketh unto men to edification, and exhortation, and comfort."*** The bible reveals that the simple gift of prophecy speaks only to edification, exhortation and comfort, nothing more. In the operation of this gift, the vessel doesn't speak judgment.

Apostle Frequency Revelator, in one of his books said,
The gift of prophecy is subject to the recipient of the gift. It is often the vehicle for the operation of other gifts. It is not for foretelling the future and not predictive by nature. When it becomes predictive, then it means it has blend with the word of wisdom or word of knowledge. The gift of prophecy is a spontaneous supernatural message from God to the believer that strengthens, encourages, and comforts. All Spirit-filled believers may move in the gift of prophecy from time to time as the Spirit wills. But note that there is no prediction, no announcement of future events, and no correction in the simple gift of prophecy.

The Prophetic Ministry

This is simply the ministry of a believer who operates in the prophetic anointing. The prophetic ministry is God's supernatural ability given to a believer to enable him to prophesy efficiently and effectively. Believers who operate at this level enter into the prophetic realm of God, using the prophetic anointing or the prophetic grace to speak forth the mind of God. At this point, it is necessary to state that majority of the thoughts of a believer are prophetic. But when you give yourself to the word and prayers, it can grow to an extent that every bit of our thoughts becomes prophetic. Now, also note that the believer operating the prophetic ministry doesn't automatically become a prophet. However, if they train themselves very well, they can even operate better in the prophetic than the person who is really called into the prophetic office. The prophetic ministry can give predictions, direction and judgment, but that authority of a prophet will still be absent.

The sons of the prophets in 2Kings 2, are a good example of people in the prophetic ministry. They were not yet a prophet, but were able to see, through the prophetic grace, that Elijah was to be taken away that very day. The people who operate in this realm are not prophets, but they enjoy the prophetic grace alongside their calling or ministry.

The Office of a Prophet

He that descended is the same also that ascended up far above all heavens, that he might fill all things.) And he gave some, apostles; and some, prophets; and some, evangelists; and some, pastors and teachers; For the perfecting of the saints, for the work of the ministry, for the edifying of the body of Christ: Till we all come in the unity of the faith, and of the knowledge of the Son of God, unto a perfect man, unto the measure of the stature of the fulness of Christ:

Ephesians 4:10 – 13

The office of a prophet is one of the five ministry gifts mentioned in the bible passage above. A person who is fully called into the prophetic office is called a prophet. The person in the prophetic office have all the other streams of prophecy combined together, flowing through them. They are seated in the realm and carry the full authority of that office. They carry a stronger influence, stronger authority and a stronger anointing of that realm.

Prophets are not just made, they are born. The office of the prophet is an extension of the government of Jesus on earth. It is God who train prophets and He does this through disappointments, trials and several tests, because a man who God will greatly use, He will greatly disappoint. This office is used by God in the area of rebuke, guidance, judgement, instruction, and revelation.

In one of his teachings, apostle Frequency said,
"The prophet is called to use all his visions and wisdom to draw the people unto maturity in Christ. He or she is not supposed to be a spiritual police officer who goes about finding what is wrong with people but a minister of love and compassion who reveals God's plan and purpose for people's lives in agreement with the Word of God. Now Since every believer in the New Testament have the Holy Spirit, we do not depend on prophets for direction like the Old Testament saints but we depend upon the Holy Spirit (Romans.8:14). However, the Holy Spirit still uses the prophets for us today where and when necessary but even then what they say must not contradict the Bible and the inward witness of the Holy Spirit in us. It must not drive us into confusion but must align with

God's plan and purpose for our lives. New Testament Prophets are not to provide revelations that contradict the Bible and they are not to be people of bad temperament, cursing and calling fire on people. Elijah shouldn't be their role model but Jesus Christ who is the perfection of compassionate (2 Kings 1:10; Luke 9:54-56). Ephesians. 4:12 explains that all the ministry gifts are given for the perfecting of the saints. So, they will be necessary for as long as the church is not yet perfect."

This teaching above is very important and is one that every prophet must read over and over again and it must sink into his heart. A prophet doesn't go around becoming the Holy Spirit in the life of people. As much as the office of the prophet is important, so also we must not fall into the temptation of shifting people's focus on ourselves. This is a very common temptation of the prophet.

People will want to make you their God, do not allow that to happen. Because majority of the believer cannot hear God clearly for themselves, they therefore love to be around anyone who hears God. Do not let this enter into your mind and open you up to temptations from the devil. You will be tempted to want to take over their thinking and life. Because they believe you are very close to God and that you hear God more than them, whatever you tell them is what they would want to do. Hence, the devil will want to tempt you into making yourself their God. Don't fall for that temptation; avoid it like cancer. You are to show them how to see and hear God, not how to see and hear you. You are to teach them how to become like Christ, not how to become like you.

In 1Corinthians 11: 1 Paul said, ***"Be ye followers of me, even as I also am of Christ."*** He never said, follow me and forget Christ.

5

SECRETS OF THE PROPHETIC: HOW TO RECEIVE A PROPHETIC WORD

Receiving a prophetic word is very easy and simple. The reason why many are finding it difficult to operate this is that they sometimes place too much demand on themselves. We expect to see a big cloud appear where a voice will be speaking and then letters begin to fly all around, or we want to see a mighty angel drop from heaven and then begin to dictates names, addresses, numbers etc, to us. As much as those things are possible, also know that prophetic words don't always come like that. Truly an angel can appear to you and begin to speak to you, but it cannot always be like that.

Sometimes ago, I was giving a prophetic word for someone. While the person was standing before me, it was like a paper was place in the person's chest and I was reading the messages from there. But I won't lie to you, ever since then, I have never had such experience again – over nine years now. But yes, I have received powerful prophecies by other means. What I'm trying to say is that God cannot be narrowed down or restricted to a corner.

In this chapter, I will mention the common ways through which prophetic messages can be received.

Delivery of Prophetic Words

Before I go into that, let me quickly talk about the process by which prophecies must be delivered, in order to avoid mistakes. You don't want to make mistakes in the prophetic and then put yourself and your ministry in the danger of being called a false prophet or your ministry tagged a false ministry.

Delivery of a prophetic word is on three levels: *Revelation, interpretation and application.* All these three must be well attended to and you cannot attend to them very well if you don't learn to ask questions from Holy Spirit.

Revelation is the message given you by the Holy Spirit, interpretation is the divine meaning of the revelation you have been given and application is how to use the revelation you have received. Or let me put it like this: Revelation answers the question, *"Father, what do you have to tell me about so and so situation?"* Interpretation answers the question, *"Father, what is the meaning of what you have shown me?"* While application answers the question, *"Father, what do I do with the interpretation you just gave me?"* Don't assume you know the meaning until you ask for it. Take this golden advice, ***"always rely on God for the interpretation and application of any revelation you receive from Him."***

One of my lecturers in the bible college told us the story of a pastor who saw in a vision that he would have six wives. He woke up, knowing very well that God have spoken to him and went on to take in another wife. After some years, he already had four wives and the house became a boxing ring, quarrels among the wives and children was a daily routine in the home which used to be very peaceful when he had only one wife. One day, he was coming from a ministration and several meters away, he was hearing noises oozing from his house, he turned around and went to look for a secluded place to cry to God about it, blaming God for giving him an instruction that have torn his home and ministry apart and have also taken away his peace. Then, God told him, that he actually misinterpreted the dream he had. The meaning of the six wives he saw was actually six branches of his church. God was trying to tell him that within few years he would have five more branches added to his church, making it six branches altogether. But because he didn't bother to ask what his dream meant, he took it to mean that he was going to have six wives.

You see, don't just assume you know the meaning of a vision given to you, endeavour to ask the One who gave you the vision, for its interpretation and application. This is a first class counsel. You don't want to put a question mark on yourself and your ministry.

That said, now I will go into various ways through which God gives prophetic words. Get ready to start prophesying!!!

Dreams

Yes, prophecies can be received through dreams. I have received a lot of direct and straightforward prophecies through dreams on several occasions. Dream is a replay of what God have dropped into your spirit which is needed to be moved into your mind, but maybe because you have been too busy to pick the message, it will then be played to you in your dream. Also sometimes, when the prophecy is one that is very detailed and must be fully captured and you have not yet trained yourself to flow very well in seeing visions, that information will be brought to you in your dream in the form of moving pictures or like a movie.

Here, you must note that dreams are often full of signs and symbols; they are usually given in parables, hence they must not be interpreted literally. If you look at the book of Daniel, you will see several pointers to the fact that God do speak through dreams and that dreams can come with numerous signs and symbols. Through a dream, God spoke to Pharaoh about a sore famine that was coming on the land and Joseph was able to interpret (Genesis 41).

Visions

Visions can either be received with your eyes closed or with your eyes open. There are closed visions and there are open visions. Closed visions are the visions we see while our eyes are closed. You are not sleeping, you're fully awake but your eyes are closed. It is usually come in the form of an imagination. As you close your eyes, you ask God what He has to say and then break into your imagination and be still. Every first picture or visions that appear is always correct. It can come in form of pictures or like seeing a movie. The picture can either be still or moving. When this is seen, it is important that you ask for the meaning of what is shown to you in order to avoid the mistake of misinterpreting what you saw. This is because the interpretation of a vision is much more important than the vision itself, like I said earlier.

Open visions come the same way as closed vision, just that you receive it with your eyes wide open. You're fully conscious of yourself and your environment, but at the same time, you're seeing into the realm of the spirit. The gift of discerning of spirits, functions in this realm very well.

Prophetic Flashback

When you look at a person and ask the Holy Spirit for a prophetic word for him or her, an information about someone you used to know (maybe someone you haven't seen a long time) may flow through your mind, this means that the person you are prophesying to, have something to do with the same information that entered your mind; this is called prophetic flashback. Sometimes, when you ask God about the name of the person standing before you, the name of someone you use to know drops in your mind, this may mean that the person standing before you bears the same name. It often come in the form of some random thoughts. For instance when you receive a word of knowledge concerning people with illnesses, it could come like a random thought about someone you know, that was just healed of the same ailment. Also, don't forget to always ask God for the meaning of a message you've received.

Body Signs

This is a situation whereby a prophetic word is given through body signs. You might be ministering to someone and suddenly, you start having strange feelings in your body. It may mean that the person you're talking to is having health issues related to the feeling you're having.

Sometimes ago, I was in a programme and as I was ministering, I started feeling a strong heaviness in my right arm. A feeling like I was having a bone fracture. Then I knew it was about somebody in the congregation. Then I said, "there is somebody here, you're having pains in your right arm, like a bone fracture", then a woman from the congregation stood up with POP on her right arm. That is an example of a revelation given through body signs. You can be ministering and you will start having strong headache, it means someone in the congregation is suffering from migraine or any head related disease.

Pay Attention to Clues

Sometimes God gives us clue to specific information about people, sometimes if a person is Samuel all of a sudden you may start thinking about Samuel in the bible, the you will know you are prophesying to a person called Samuel. Look at someone, take a snapshot of the person and put it in your imagination. Keep looking at it in your mind and be still and relaxed. The picture will change and the revelation will start flowing.

Audible Voice

You can audibly hear prophetic messages by instrument of the Holy Spirit. You will clearly hear Him speaking to your ears. Know that audible voice is not a voice from outside, it is actually coming from within because the Holy Spirit is not speaking from outside but from within your spirit. This voice is not forceful or pushy. This is the area that most people want start operating from. But the truth is that it doesn't come often. You have to grow into it.

The Five Senses

The five senses that is, the eye, the nose, the ear, taste and feelings, can be used of God to communicate prophetic messages to you. While standing before someone you may begin to perceive some smell, this is pointer to the prophetic message that is needed to be delivered.

For example, sometimes ago I was praying for a man of God and I began to perceive some fowl odour from nowhere, immediately I asked the Holy Spirit what it means, and I heard the word "family". Which means the man in question was having marital crises. At that time, I never knew about it because he wasn't someone I'm close to. But few years later the man's wife divorced him. This is a perfect illustration that God can use our senses to communicate to us.

Sometimes, you can start perceiving the smell of a rose flower, which is actually signifying a wedding or you can start perceiving the smell of rusted iron, this also, indicate that the person is in a long term battle or problem. You can also begin to see colours. Colours can be used to convey a prophetic word: pale or fading colour means death, black usually means evil, blue means something heavenly etc. Also, numbers can be used: three means unity, seven means perfection, nine means fruitfulness etc. You can lay hands on prophetic books that teach meaning of colours and numbers.

Prophetic Impressions

Prophetic impressions are very powerful tool to receiving prophetic messages. It comes in the form of strong thoughts that were not premeditated. It will not be a preconceived thought but rather a supernatural knowing of details and facts that you wouldn't have naturally known except you were told. Many of the thoughts that come to our mind are actually God speaking to us, but because we don't trust them or because we have not trained ourselves very well in that direction, we miss that word from God.

Prophetic Activator

This is very important also and I must talk about it. It is when God uses something on the body of the person, to speak to you about them. Whenever you stand in front of a person to give them a word of knowledge, ask God for prophetic activator. As you are looking at the person, the Lord will highlight something on the person (it could be the hair, the clothe, the shoe, the belt, or any part of their body), keep looking at that thing while you ask the Holy Spirit what He was trying to communicate to you. Pay attention to the first thought that came to your mind – the fist thought is always correct. That part of the body or wears that was used to convey the message to you is what I call a prophetic activator. It can be used to set the prophetic flow in motion.

6

ANGELS AND THE PROPHETIC MINISTRY

This duo is inseparable. The prophetic and angelic experiences work hand in hand. In fact, it is impossible to be a true prophet without having angelic experiences. No major prophets mentioned in the bible lacked angelic ministrations. Our Lord Jesus Christ did not lack this wonderful ministry. Talk of Elisha, Elijah, Peter, Paul, John etc.

Every believer in Christ is entitled to angelic ministrations but that of the prophet is usually on a different level. Angelic traffic around prophets is usually very high. Sometimes, you will need angels to give accurate and forensic prophecies; you will need strong warring angels to fend off demonic attacks because Satan will hurl attacks against you. You must also know that angels will not just come around if not sent by God or invited by you. Some angels will stay permanently with you while some will be coming and going.

The prophetic need a heavy presence of angels and it is very important to know this truth. Many today, will not give the total truth to their listeners. They tell you what God will do for you through grace regardless of how you live and your level of character, obedience, and consecration. Angels don't stay around believers who live in unrepentant sinful nature. We tend to forget about those angels. They are mighty. They are enormous in strength and hearken to the voice of God's Word (see Ps. 103:20). They are sent by the Lord to minister to us, but very often our lack of consecration limits them.

Notice how angels ministered to Jesus after He overcame the temptations of Satan in the wilderness (Matt. 4:11). Every time Jesus was tempted He spoke the Word of God. That's what the angels hearken to. But what we fail to often see about these verses is the consecration that Jesus made at the beginning of His ministry. He spent 40 days and nights in prayer and fasting and overcame every temptation the devil threw at Him. The angels then came and ministered to Him.

"Be gone, Satan! For it is written, 'You shall worship the Lord your God, and serve Him only.' Then the devil left Him; and behold, angels came and began to minister to Him"

Matthew 4:10 – 11

That word 'minister' generally means to do anyone a service and care for someone's needs. Here's something we may not have seen before. Angels are not only committed to the Lord and His Word, they are committed to those who speak His Word and obey it. In a certain sense angels are drawn to the prophet's consecration and their surrender to the Lord's will.

Notice another example of how angels ministered to Jesus at the end of His ministry in the garden of Gethsemane as Jesus battled to fulfill and complete our redemption. Once again we know what a difficult trial this was for Jesus.

In the garden He prayed the same prayer of consecration three times as Matthew recorded it, and so intense was the struggle that Jesus' sweat was like great drops of blood (Matt. 26:44). We see here one more time the correlation between the angels and the consecration Jesus made. Angels honor the word of the Lord and they are activated by a prophet's consecration and reverence for God's word.

How angels minister to/for a prophet

Angels minister to believers in diverse ways on different level. But here, I will mention just few of those ways.

Defense

One of the ministries of angels is in the area of protection. Angels are sent to minister defense just as they can be offensive to the enemies. The bible says,

"The angel of the LORD encampeth round about them that fear him, and delivereth them."

Psalm 34:7.

This is very important to the prophetic ministry because the prophetic ministry is one that is always under a spiritual attack. Because you are setting people free from demonic bondages, don't expect the devil to just keep looking at you. He will surely come for you and that's why angels are around to fight the spiritual battles on our behalf.

Interpretation of dreams and visions

Angels are wise creatures and they often help in interpretation of dreams and visions. They also have an understanding of signs and symbols and they help to give knowledge in this area when we engage them. This important ministry of angels cannot be side tracked in the prophetic because it helps us not to live in confusion. If you look through the bible from Genesis to Revelation, you will see lots of instances where angels helped men and women of God to interpret dreams and visions. This kind of angelic ministry is well documented in the book of Daniel.

See this account of Daniel chapter 10,

1 In the third year of Cyrus king of Persia a thing was revealed unto Daniel, whose name was called Belteshazzar; and the thing was true, but the time appointed was long: and he understood the thing, and had understanding of the vision.

2 In those days I Daniel was mourning three full weeks.

3 I ate no pleasant bread, neither came flesh nor wine in my mouth, neither did I anoint myself at all, till three whole weeks were fulfilled.

4 And in the four and twentieth day of the first month, as I was by the side of the great river, which is Hiddekel;

5 Then I lifted up mine eyes, and looked, and behold a certain man clothed in linen, whose loins were girded with fine gold of Uphaz:

6 His body also was like the beryl, and his face as the appearance of lightning, and his eyes as lamps of fire, and his arms and his feet like in colour to polished brass, and the voice of his words like the voice of a multitude.

7 And I Daniel alone saw the vision: for the men that were with me saw not the vision; but a great quaking fell upon them, so that they fled to hide themselves.

8 Therefore I was left alone, and saw this great vision, and there remained no strength in me: for my comeliness was turned in me into corruption, and I retained no strength.

9 Yet heard I the voice of his words: and when I heard the voice of his words, then was I in a deep sleep on my face, and my face toward the ground.

10 And, behold, an hand touched me, which set me upon my knees and upon the palms of my hands.

11 And he said unto me, O Daniel, a man greatly beloved, understand the words that I speak unto thee, and stand upright: for unto thee am I now sent. And when he had spoken this word unto me, I stood trembling.

12 Then said he unto me, Fear not, Daniel: for from the first day that thou didst set thine heart to understand, and to chasten thyself before thy God, thy words were heard, and I am come for thy words.

13 But the prince of the kingdom of Persia withstood me one and twenty days: but, lo, Michael, one of the chief princes, came to help me; and I remained there with the kings of Persia.

14 Now I am come to make thee understand what shall befall thy people in the latter days: for yet the vision is for many days.

15 And when he had spoken such words unto me, I set my face toward the ground, and I became dumb.

16 And, behold, one like the similitude of the sons of men touched my lips: then I opened my mouth, and spake, and

said unto him that stood before me, O my lord, by the vision my sorrows are turned upon me, and I have retained no strength.

17 For how can the servant of this my lord talk with this my lord? for as for me, straightway there remained no strength in me, neither is there breath left in me.

18 Then there came again and touched me one like the appearance of a man, and he strengthened me,

19 And said, O man greatly beloved, fear not: peace be unto thee, be strong, yea, be strong. And when he had spoken unto me, I was strengthened, and said, Let my lord speak; for thou hast strengthened me.

20 Then said he, Knowest thou wherefore I come unto thee? and now will I return to fight with the prince of Persia: and when I am gone forth, lo, the prince of Grecia shall come.

21 But I will shew thee that which is noted in the scripture of truth: and there is none that holdeth with me in these things, but Michael your prince.

So, it is very clear that angelic ministry help in interpretation of dreams and visions. They can appear in dreams and visions. Also note that angels of darkness can come too, but the best way to know an angel is from the Lord is that he will not give you an interpretation that contradicts the scripture.

Word of knowledge

The gift of word of knowledge is a part of the prophetic ministry. The gift of the word of knowledge is the supernatural ability to see into the past. There are angels that help in giving knowledge about past events in the lives of people.

Encouragement

Angels also help in giving encouragement.
"Then the devil leaveth him, and, behold, angels came and ministered unto him." – Matthew 4:11. During hard times, temptations etc, angels are agents that God can use to give us encouragements or give words of comfort.

21 But after long abstinence Paul stood forth in the midst of them, and said, Sirs, ye should have hearkened unto me, and not have loosed from Crete, and to have gained this harm and loss.

22 And now I exhort you to be of good cheer: for there shall be no loss of any man's life among you, but of the ship.

23 For there stood by me this night the angel of God, whose I am, and whom I serve,

24 Saying, Fear not, Paul; thou must be brought before Caesar: and, lo, God hath given thee all them that sail with thee.

25 Wherefore, sirs, be of good cheer: for I believe God, that it shall be even as it was told me.

Acts 27:21 - 25

7

THE PROPHETIC LANGUAGE

Prophetic dreams and visions often come with signs and symbols and if these things are not well interpreted, we may miss the main message that was to be passed across, hence, the importance of learning and understanding prophetic languages. I call it prophetic language because they are languages that are commonly used in disseminating prophetic dreams, visions and revelations to man. It is the language by which prophecies are given or delivered.

When we go through the books of the bible, we would see places where God gave visions and revelations that are filled with symbols and signs. This is because we serve a speaking God who really loves to communicate His mind to us, but because of our limited knowledge and understanding, God have to use earthly things that we are familiar with, to communicate divine information to us. This is because heaven language cannot be really understood by man because of man's nature.

This chapter will help you to understand these prophetic symbols and you can easily be a mouth piece of God in your territory. I gathered this information from many years of experience and study on the prophetic.

In order to easily understand Prophecies, we must firstly acquaint ourselves with the figurative language of the prophets. This language is taken from the analogy between the natural world, and an empire or kingdom we call the government of the world. The prophetic language is God's way of using the visible things we can see to give prophecies. This is when God uses the human language to describe a future event.

Jeremiah 1: 11 – 14

11 Moreover the word of the LORD came unto me, saying, Jeremiah, what seest thou? And I said, I see a rod of an almond tree.

12 Then said the LORD unto me, Thou hast well seen: for I will hasten my word to perform it.

13 And the word of the LORD came unto me the second time, saying, What seest thou? And I said, I see a seething pot; and the face thereof is toward the north.

14 Then the LORD said unto me, Out of the north an evil shall break forth upon all the inhabitants of the land.

Here we see how God was testing the spiritual sight of the young prophet Jeremiah. God was using things that Jeremiah was familiar with to explain to him what His intent was. This is a perfect example of a prophetic language.

I could remember sometimes ago around 2013/2014, I saw in a revelation that there was a heavy earthquake that stretched over the land of Ikere Ekiti, a town in the western part of Nigeria. After about one month, the king of that town died. In the prophetic language, an earthquake that stretches across a land is often a sign of a government passing away or a change of government.

Later, I also saw that water arose from the sea and flooded a particular market in that same town such that people could not go to that market place to either sell or buy. Then after about five days, the chief in charge of that street where the market was located died and the market was closed indefinitely till another chief was installed. It is the custom of that land that whenever that chief dies, the market must be closed down till another chief is installed.

So, you can see how God used what I'm familiar with to show me, in a revelation, what was about to happen. That is a perfect illustration to describe the concept of prophetic language.

Some Biblical Prophetic Languages

What I am about to share in this section is what I gathered from some of my research on the interpretation of dreams and visions and also in my desire to have a better understanding of the prophetic language. I see the truth shared in this section as very correct and systematic. I saw this information in one of the numerous books I have come across on prophetic language and I have applied them personally on various occasions and they have been very accurate. So, let's get to see this together.

- The heavens and the things in it, signify thrones and dignities, and those who enjoy them.
- The earth, with the things on it, signifies the inferior people.
- Ascending towards heaven, and descending to the earth, means rising and falling in power and honor.
- Rising out of the earth, or waters, and falling into them, means rising up to any dignity or dominion, out of the

inferior state of the people, or falling down from the same into that inferior state;.

- Descending into the lower parts of the earth, means descending to a very low and unhappy estate.
- Speaking with a faint voice out of the dust, means being in a weak and low condition.
- Moving from one place to another means translation from one office, dignity, or dominion, to another.
- Great earthquakes and the shaking of heaven and earth, means the shaking of kingdoms, so as to distract or overthrow them (you can see this in the illustration from personal experience that I used above).
- The creating of a new heaven and earth, and the passing away of an old one, or the beginning and end of the world, means the rise and ruin of the institution signified by it.

Prophetic Language using the heavenly bodies

- The Sun and Moon means Kings and Queens. But in sacred Prophecy. The Sun can also mean a specie and race of Kings, while the Moon would mean the common people.

- When the Sun is Christ, the moon would mean the church and the stars would mean Bishops and Rulers of the people of God. Light often means glory, truth, and knowledge, with which great and good men shine and illuminate others. Darkness means error, blindness and ignorance.
- Darkening or setting of the Sun, Moon, and Stars, usually means the ceasing of a kingdom. Darkening the Sun, turning the Moon into blood, and falling of the Stars, also mean the same thing. While new moons means the return of a dispersed people or the restoration of something that was long lost.

Prophetic Language using Fire and meteors

- Burning anything with fire means signify war.
- A conflagration of the earth, or turning a country into a lake of fire, means consumption of a kingdom by war.

- Being in a furnace means being in slavery under another nation or a strange government either spiritual or physical.
- The ascending up of the smoke of any burning thing forever and ever, is means the continuation of a conquered people under the misery of perpetual subjection and slavery.
- The scorching heat of the sun means vexations, persecutions and troubles.
- Riding on the clouds, means reigning over much people.
- Covering the sun with a cloud, or with smoke, means for oppression by the armies of an enemy.
- Thunder or the voice of a cloud, means the voice of a multitude.
- A storm of thunder, lightning, hail, and overflowing rain, means a tempest of war descending from the heavens and clouds, on the heads of an enemy.
- Rain [if moderate], dew and living water, means the graces and doctrines of the Spirit while the defect of rain, would mean spiritual barrenness.

Prophetic Language using the earthly bodies

- The dry land and congregated waters such as a sea, a river, a flood, means people of several regions or tribes, nations, and dominions.
- Embittering of waters means great affliction of people by war and persecution.
- Turning things into blood means mystical death of government bodies, that is, for their dissolution.
- The overflowing of a sea or river means the invasion of an institution's government, by the people of the waters.
- Drying up of waters means the conquest of a region by the earth.
- A fountain of waters, mountains and islands means the cities of the earth.
- Dens and rocks of mountains, means the temples in cities.
- The hiding of men in those dens and rocks means the shutting up of Idols in their temples.
- Houses and ships, means families, assemblies, and towns, in the earth and and a navy of ships of war,

means an army of that kingdom which is signified by the sea.

Prophetic Language using animals and vegetables

- Animals also and vegetables means people of several regions and conditions and particularly, trees, herbs, and land animals, means the people of the earth.
- A forest means a kingdom and a wilderness means a desolate and thin people.
- If the world government, considered in the prophetic dream and vision, consists of many kingdoms, they are represented by as many parts of the natural world as possible.

Prophetic Language using a Beast or Man to represent a kingdom

- His parts and qualities are parts and qualities of the kingdom it was used to represent.
- The head of a Beast represents the great men who precede and govern that kingdom.

- The tail represents the inferior people, who follow and are governed.
- The heads, if more than one, represents the number of capital parts, or dynasties, or dominions in the kingdom, whether collateral or successive, with respect to the civil government.
- The horns on any head, represents the number of kingdoms in that head, with respect to military power.
- Sight represents understanding while the eyes represents men of understanding and policy, and in matters of religion it is used for Bishops/overseers.
- Speaking represents making laws.
- The mouth represents a law-giver, whether civil or sacred.
- The loudness of the voice represents might and power while faintness of the voice is put for weakness.
- Eating and drinking, represents acquiring what is signified by what is being eaten and drank.
- The hairs of a beast, or man, and the feathers of a bird, represent people.

- The wings, represents the number of kingdoms represented by the beast.
- The arm of a man is put for his power, or for any people wherein his strength and power consists.
- His feet represent the lowest of the people, or for the latter end of the kingdom.
- The feet, nails, and teeth of beasts or prey, are put for armies and squadrons of armies.
- The bones, represents strength, and for fortified places.
- The flesh, represents riches and possessions.
- The days of their acting, represents years.
- When a tree is put for a kingdom, its branches, leaves, and fruit, means the same thing as the wings, feathers, and food of a bird or beast.

When a man is taken in a mystical sense, his qualities are often signified by his actions, and by the circumstances of things about him.

- So a Ruler is signified by his riding on a beast;
- A Warrior and Conqueror, is signified by his having a sword and bow;
- A potent man is signified by his gigantic stature;

- A Judge is signified by weights and measures;
- A sentence of absolution, or condemnation, is signified by a white or a black stone;
- A new dignity is signified by a new name;
- Moral or civil qualifications, is signified by garments;
- Honor and glory, is signified by splendid apparel;
- Royal dignity is signified by purple or scarlet, or by a crown;
- Righteousness is signified by white and clean robes;
- Wickedness is signified by spotted and filthy garments;
- Affliction, mourning, and humiliation, is signified by clothing in sackcloth;
- Dishonor, shame, and want of good works, is signified by nakedness;
- Error and misery, is signified by drinking a cup of his or her wine that causes it;
- Propagating any religion for gain, is signified by exercising traffic and merchandise with that people whose religion it is;

- Worshiping or serving the false Gods of any nation is signified by committing adultery with their princes, or by worshiping them;
- A Council of a kingdom is signified by its image;
- Idolatry is signified by blasphemy;
- Overthrow in war, is signified by a wound of man or beast;
- A durable plague of war, is signified by a sore and pain;
- The affliction or persecution which a people suffers in laboring to bring forth a new kingdom, is signified by the pain of a woman in labor to bring forth a man-child;
- The dissolution of a body politic or ecclesiastic is signified by the death of a man or beast;
- The revival of a dissolved dominion is signified by the resurrection of the dead.

All these prophetic language compiled in this chapter are not self discoveries, but rather what I read from other books as well and have really helped me a lot. I own no right to them but I included it in this book because I see that it will help anyone develop a sharper understanding of prophetic signs and symbols.

8

7 MISTAKES YOU MUST AVOID IN THE PROPHETIC

Many prophets miss the plan of God for their ministry because they ran into error. I have seen great prophets who are now silent just because of some mistakes that they made in their ministry. Of all the ministry gifts, the prophetic is the one that can easily veer into error. The line between the prophetic and error or erroneous practices is very thin, hence the need for a prophet to be very careful and never spend a single moment away from the presence of the Lord.

In this chapter, I will highlight few but most important mistakes you must avoid as a prophetic person.

1. Don't assume you know the meaning of a revelation until you have ask God

This is a great mistake that many prophets make. Don't be in a hurry to deliver a prophecy or a word of knowledge - ask God first. The meaning might not be what you think. God cannot be caged to a point. What the vision of a rose flower means to one person's life might be different from what it means to the life of another person. So that you will not open yourself up to demonic deceptions, learn to ask questions.

2. **Avoid show offs**

Rather pursue to glorify God with the prophetic. Don't fall under pressure to prophesy – your peace is key. Don't fall victim of pressures from your congregation. The primary duty of the ministry is to teach men and build them to the full stature of Christ. Major more on building the people, not on showing off the gift. Christ must be lifted and glorified.

3. You are to call gold out of people

Don't go about looking for people's mistakes and sins. Of course the Holy Ghost will show you the deep things about people. You will be able to see secret sins that people have refused to repent from, but the purpose for which you were allowed to see it is not to condemn them, but to help them come out of it. Also know that it is not everything that you must speak into the microphone. Sometimes, you have to take away the mic and say speak to the person as softly as possible.

Don't embarrass people with their sins. If God didn't do it, you should not do it either. Learn to call gold out of people, so that the door of the prophetic will not be closed against you.

4. The prophetic lives on the other side of fear

Many who should've become great prophets have been limited because of the fear of, *"what if I miss?"* Why don't you want to miss? We have all missed it at one point or the other and we are still missing. You are not the first to miss and you will not be the last to. Don't be afraid to step out, don't be afraid of prophesying. Step out in faith and kill that fear.

5. Don't start with calling names and addresses

Don't start out as a young prophet by calling names, numbers and addresses. The truth is that you will surely miss, because those are realms we grow into. We don't start prophesying from there. It is like starting to build a house from the roof without laying the foundation. God is not in a hurry for you to grow, why are you in a hurry? Calm down and start small. Do not despise the days of little beginning.

6. Don't major on your mistakes

You say five things and the person confirms only three, forget about the ones that are not accurate, focus on the ones that are accurate. We all make mistakes because we are not God. You don't have to go into depression because you missed. Focus on the correct one and later, you can sit down and reason on why you missed.

7. Don't throw away your pray and bible study habit

If you don't want the devil to take over your gift, don't joke with your prayer life. Your relationship with the Holy Spirit is number one. This is what has led many into grave mistakes and untimely death. Don't make the mistake of relying on the gift and then leave your personal relationship with the Holy Spirit. This is a golden counsel.

AUTHOR'S PROFILE

Samuel Akindahunsi is a Prophet of God, with a divine mandate to minister the gospel of our Lord Jesus Christ to the nations of the world. He is the founder and president of *Royal Message Ministries (RMM)* – a global evangelical outreach ministry with the mandate to raise believers into the full stature of Christ through sound biblical teachings and also taking the gospel round the world through open air evangelical outreaches/crusades and local assembly revivals. He had pastored eight different churches for several years before obeying the call to proceed with Royal Message Ministries.

He has been to many villages, town and cities across Nigeria on evangelical outreaches and church meetings and still pressing on with the work of the ministry.

Made in the USA
Columbia, SC
30 June 2025